Green Pea

Makes A Flourless Cookie

Keep Smiley *To Alisha*

Author
Chance Hansen

Illustrator
Pascha Hansen

Printed in the United States of America.

ISBN: 978-1-4669-2637-0 (sc)
978-1-4669-2638-7 (e)

Library of Congress Control Number: 2012906176

Trafford rev. 07/28/2012

 www.trafford.com

North America & international
toll-free: 1 888 232 4444 (USA & Canada)
phone: 250 383 6864 ♦ fax: 812 355 4082

THANK YOU

I would like to thank the Creator for guiding me through this new life.

To my mom and business partner, Pascha Hansen, for making another book possible and for your support through this.

To Granny and Granddad for all their support.

Green Pea and I would like to thank you, too!

One day Green Pea wanted to bake cookies. Green Pea first needed Nut Butter, Eggs, Brown Sugar and Chocolate Chips.

FLOURLESS COOKIE

2 CUPS BROWN SUGAR

2 EGGS

I CUP PEANUT BUTTER

I CUP ALMOND BUTTER

1/2   I CUP CHOCOLATE CHIPS

OVEN 350 DEGREES FAHRENHEIT

       180 DEGREES CELSIUS

10-12 MINUTES

Green Pea went and collected two eggs from a chicken.

CLUCK

CLUCK

Green Pea then went to the store and bought brown sugar, almonds, peanuts and chocolate.

CHACHING

CHACHING

Green Pea then put on
his bakers hair net
and washed his hands.

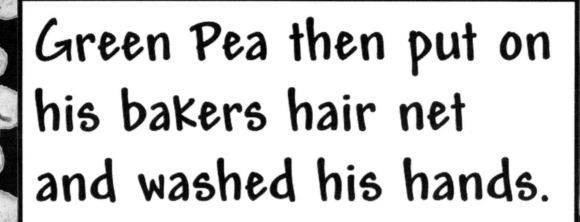

Green Pea crushed
almonds and peanuts
until he made nut
butter.

CRUNCH

CRUNCH

Green Pea then placed the two cups of brown sugar into the bowl.

SWOOSH SWOOSH

Brown Sugar

Green Pea then cracked two eggs into the bowl.

CRACK

CRACK

Green Pea then placed two cups of sticky nut butter into the bowl.

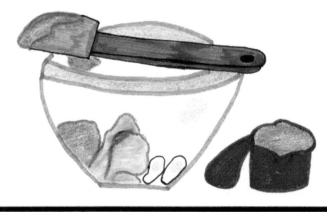

Green Pea then poured some sweet chocolate chips into the bowl.

TINKLE

TINKLE

Green Pea then mixed all the ingredients together.

SWISH

SWISH

Green Pea then shaped the cookie dough into round balls and flattened them on a baking sheet.

SQUISH SQUISH

Mother Pea then placed the cookies in the oven to bake for about ten minutes at 180 degrees Celsius, 350 degrees Fahrenheit.

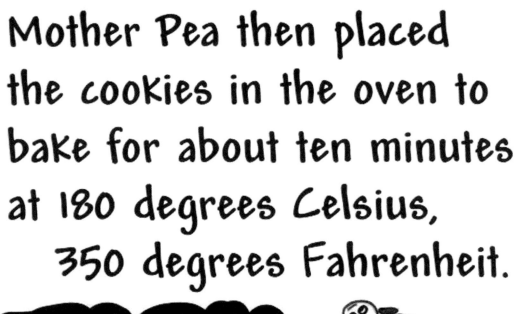

After a while Mother Pea took the warm tasty cookies out of the oven and let them cool on a plate.

DING DING

Our Favorites

 -sunflower seed butter & raisins

 -peanut butter & dark chocolate

 -almond butter & peanut butter

 -cashew butter

Catch More Green Pea Adventures

Green Pea, Not A Home For Me!

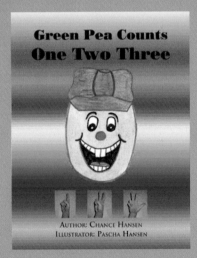

Green Pea Counts One Two Three

Coming Soon

Green Pea Sing to Me

Green Pea Goes To Salad Bowl School

CPSIA information can be obtained
at www.ICGtesting.com
Printed in the USA
LVIC040700171112

307653LV00005B